Books

CHOMPS

The really nearly deadly canoe ride

In their latest do-it-yourself
adventure, Pete 'Pod' Podlewski
and Morris 'Shiny-Boy' Diamond
attempt to canoe *all* the way
from Sockby to the sea.

But they didn't count on revolting
rubbish traps, killer rapids, freaky
whirlpools, and a container ship
ten storeys high . . .

Grab another Chomp!

The Mal Rider
Pat Flynn

Stinky Ferret and the JJs
Candice Lemon-Scott

The Really Really Epic Mini-bike Ride
David Metzenthen

The Really Really High Diving Tower
David Metzenthen

Josie & the Michael Street Kids
Penni Russon

There's Money in Toilets
Robert Greenberg

Trolley Boys
James Moloney

Boots and All
Sherryl Clark

68 Teeth
James Moloney

Aussie **CHOMPS**

The really nearly deadly canoe ride

David Metzenthen

Puffin Books

For Liam and Ella

PUFFIN BOOKS

Published by the Penguin Group
Penguin Group (Australia)
250 Camberwell Road, Camberwell, Victoria 3124, Australia
(a division of Pearson Australia Group Pty Ltd)
Penguin Group (USA) Inc.
375 Hudson Street, New York, New York 10014, USA
Penguin Group (Canada)
90 Eglinton Avenue East, Suite 700, Toronto, ON M4P 2Y3, Canada
(a division of Pearson Penguin Canada Inc.)
Penguin Books Ltd
80 Strand, London WC2R 0RL, England
Penguin Ireland
25 St Stephen's Green, Dublin 2, Ireland
(a division of Penguin Books Ltd)
Penguin Books India Pvt Ltd
11, Community Centre, Panchsheel Park, New Delhi-110 017, India
Penguin Group (NZ)
67 Apollo Drive, Rosedale, North Shore 0632, New Zealand
(a division of Pearson New Zealand Ltd)
Penguin Books (South Africa) (Pty) Ltd
24 Sturdee Avenue, Rosebank, Johannesburg 2196, South Africa

Penguin Books Ltd, Registered Offices: 80 Strand, London WC2R 0RL, England

First published by Penguin Group (Australia), 2009

1 3 5 7 9 10 8 6 4 2

Text copyright © David Metzenthen, 2009
Illustrations copyright © Jiri Tibor Novak, 2009

Cover design by Claire Wilson © Penguin Group (Australia)
Series design by David Altheim © Penguin Group (Australia)
Illustrations by Jiri Tibor Novak
Typeset in 13/21 pt Berkeley by Post Pre-press Group, Brisbane, Queensland
Printed in Australia by McPherson's Printing Group,
Maryborough, Victoria

National Library of Australia
Cataloguing-in-Publication data:

Metzenthen, David.
The really nearly deadly canoe ride / David Metzenthen.
ISBN: 978 0 14 330454 8.
Series: Aussie chomps.
Canoes and canoeing – Juvenile fiction

A823.3

puffin.com.au

Chapter 1

It's a sunny Saturday morning, and Shiny-Boy and I are up a tree in my backyard checking out the neighbourhood.

'Now *stupidly* enough, Pod,' Shiny says, making a telescope with one fist, 'I spy with my little eye something beginning with . . . K.'

I hate this game. I look down into the various backyards, all of them flat, none of them exciting, most of them filled with things that don't work anymore.

'Kennel?' I try. 'How about *Kathmandu*?' Truly,

I have no idea what Shiny's on about. Over a far-off fence I see Mrs Garbutt reaching over to take something off the clothes line next door. 'Kleptomaniac?'

'Nope,' says Shine. 'Well, yeah, she is, but that's not what I meant. Give up?'

'It looks like I might have to.'

'Canoe,' says Shine.

Oh, boy. Don't even go there, Pod, I tell myself. Do *not*.

'Where, Shine?'

'Right there.' Morris 'Shiny-Boy' Diamond points to the yard next door where old Mr Beanland is dragging a wooden canoe out of his garage.

'Nice boat, Mr B!' Shiny shouts, hanging out of the tree. 'Don't go gettin' stuck up any creeks without a paddle! Because it'll be a creek where you don't want to be!'

Mr Beanland waves. As usual, he is wearing his ancient baggy trousers held up with a piece of cord, and holey grey tennis shoes. This is his Totem Tennis outfit, a game which he used to play every day for thirty minutes for fitness, sometimes blindfolded.

'Howdy, boys.' Mr Beanland shades his eyes against the sun. 'I'm just takin' a last look at my good old canoe, the mighty *Wolverine*, before I head on back over to Canada. I can't take her with me. So here she stays, along with my Totem Tennis pole, I'm afraid. Boy, did I ever give that thing a few whacks.'

'I didn't know he was *Canadian*,' Shiny mutters. 'My mum reckoned he was from *Canberra*. Well, that truly is amazing, Pod.'

My name's Pete Podlewski. Nearly everybody calls me Pod.

'Does he sound like he's from Canberra?' I say.

'He came out here to Sockby after the war to set up a rubber band factory. He was a bomber pilot with the Canadian Air Force.'

'Well, that's freakin' me out even more.' Shine folds his arms, despite being five metres up a tree. 'I didn't even know the Canadians *had* a war against us. I always thought they *liked* Australians.'

What Shiny does and doesn't know, and pretends *not* to know, would fill a library.

'Are you going to stay in Canada, Mr Beanland?' I ask, because he used to visit his cousins in Moosejaw every Christmas, and sometimes pop over to Stinkbeetle, Alaska, for his sister's birthday.

Mr Beanland comes over to the fence, wearing a cap with a red maple leaf on it, which should've told Shiny something.

'I am.' He nods slowly, perhaps a little sadly. 'So if you fellers want a genuine handmade Canadian canoe, the *Wolverine* is all yours. Just as long as

4

you swear to me three times over that you'll steer clear of *all* sorts of trouble.'

'We'd love to have it, Mr B.' Shiny starts to climb down. 'And there'll be *no* trouble at all. And as for swearing, if that's what you want, me and Pod'll do it *all* day *every* day. Even if my mum might not like it.' Shine looks at Mr Beanland for a long moment. 'That leaf cap of yours, Mr B, did you get it from The Garden Warehouse or what?'

Chapter 2

Shiny and I carry the *Wolverine* back to the Diamonds' shed. There is plenty of space in there now because Shiny's grandpa, Grandpa Jack, sold his 1965 Holden.

'Just think, Poddy,' Shiny says, studying the *Wolverine*, 'if it was calm, we could paddle to New Zealand. They've got extinct birds and everything.'

'It might be a bit far,' I say. 'But I wouldn't mind going down the Sockby Creek. Maybe all the way to the sea. Like the Canadian explorers did. You know, in Canada, that is. Not Sockby. I saw it on TV. It was *full*-on.'

'Of course it was full-on, Poddy.' Shiny waves a wooden paddle around. 'Because the great thing about explorers is that they go *wherever* they like, and do *whatever* they want, no matter *how* stupid it is. They don't listen to *anybody*. Which probably explains why heaps of 'em fell off the edge of the earth. Which wouldn't happen today, as the earth is round now.'

There's no point going too far down this track with Shiny, so I don't.

'The Sockby Creek meets up with the Yarra River,' I say. 'Which cuts right through the middle of the city and out into the bay. We could paddle *all* the way, Shine.'

'Yep!' Shine's face is pink with enthusiasm. 'We'll call it Operation Beanland. A voyage from boring, flat, dull Sockby to the sparkling, shiny sea! For the glory of Australia and Canada and whoever else might be interested. But mainly it'll get us away from home.'

I agree with that; the more time I spend away from my place, the less weeding I have to do – as my parents are total gardening maniacs.

We rub down the dusty canoe until it glows from bow to stern, although we're not quite sure which is which.

'Grandpa Jack said to sand it back to bare timber,' says Shiny. 'Then we'll paint our totem animal on it, Poddy, and re-varnish it. The Canadian Indians were right into the totem thing. You know, like the Sioux and the Iriquois.'

'How d'you know, Shine?' I ask. 'We never did any of that at school.'

'I read it on the back of a Sugar Bix box.' Shine taps his temple. 'That's why it's called brain food,

Pod. Because every morning, as you enjoy your healthy daily Sugar Bix Fix, you learn somethin'. Did you know emus can't fly? And that elephants can do paintings – if someone supplies the brushes and paper, otherwise they struggle a bit.'

We don't eat supermarket cereal. My mum makes her own muesli. She calls it Mrs Podlewski's Secret Muesli Mix, and it tastes like dirt.

'So what's our totem animal, Shine?' I ask. 'I mean, we've only got a fish at our place, and your parrot swears like a trooper.' I hesitate over my next suggestion. 'I *guess* we could put your dog on it. Chihuahuas are pretty interesting. In a way.' Apparently they are, according to Shine.

'Well,' Shiny says, 'I would like to go with Mitzi, the truly amazing Chihuahua. But seeing Mr B's already called the canoe the *Wolverine*, it'd be bad luck to change it.' Shine wipes his nose on the collar of his shirt. 'Besides, wolverines are, like, the baddest, meanest, smackdown champions of the natural world. They're fightin' *freaks*. And Chihuahuas aren't.'

'Well, as long as Wolverines can swim,' I say. 'I agree.'

Shiny looks at me strangely. 'Of course they can swim, Pod. All animals can. Except for the Spotted Somalian Desert Trotting Pig. And that's probably because no one's ever really bothered to check.'

Strangely enough.

Grandpa Jack always helps us with our projects. He lets us use his tools and shed, and he'll show us how to do things if we don't know. He'll even buy stuff for us if we're broke. Like sandpaper and varnish from the Sockby Hotel and Hardware Store.

'Boys should be boys and run wild,' is one of Grandpa Jack's favourite sayings.

When Shiny asks him what girls should be, he says, 'A good-looking cook whose old man owns a brewery.'

But Grandpa Jack doesn't mean this, because Grandma Rose, who died, was a terrible cook, her dad didn't own a brewery, and when *she* ran wild everyone got out of *her* way, including Grandpa Jack, and he's an ex-commando.

Shiny pokes one of the *Wolverine's* seats, which Mr Beanland said were woven from buffalo hide and need replacing.

'Grandpa Jack says us Diamonds have always liked exploring.' Shiny points to a photo on the shed wall of a man wearing two pairs of glasses and a hat made of leaves. 'That old guy is our great, great, grand-Uncle – Uncle 'Clever' Trevor Diamond. He helped organise the last Burke and Wills expedition, Pod. And look what they achieved.'

'They died, Shine,' I say. 'Stranded out in the desert.'

Shiny looks surprised. 'Did they? Well, that wouldn't have had anything to do with good old Uncle Trevor, as he was only in charge of packing the billiard table and the extension ladders. Anyway, Pod, think of Captain Cook. He discovered Australia, and then went to Hawaii for a holiday. So exploring is, like, a really fun thing.'

I thought Hawaii was where Captain Cook was speared to death?

'But – '

Shiny holds up a hand. He's drawn a picture of a wolverine on his palm.

'No buts about it, Pod. The wolverine spirit lives on. And we will follow it from the mountains to the sea, like you said, via the Sockby Creek and the sparkling Yarra River.'

Sockby's actually as flat as a pancake, and the

12

Yarra isn't the sparkliest river in the world, but I'm sure we can still find ourselves some sort of action or trouble. We usually do.

'You and me, Shine,' I say, and we tap fists. 'From Sockby to the sea.'

Shiny nods, dreadlocks swinging.

'You betcha, Podster. Uncle Trev'd be proud. He *lived* for adventure. He just *laughed* in the face of danger. His motto was, "Be as brave as a lion. And always take a raincoat." '

'That's inspirational, Shine,' I say.

'Really?' Shine's eyebrows dip down. 'I thought it was rubbish. Umbrellas make much more sense.'

It's probably a good thing no one gets to hear most of our conversations. In fact, I'm sure it is.

Chapter 3

With Grandpa Jack's help, Shine and I sand the canoe, and re-string the seats with some soft old rope. Then we make a tracing of a wolverine that will go on both sides of the bow.

'The great thing about wolverines,' Shine says, using a permanent marker to outline it, 'is that they're really snarly *all* the time. They've even been known to fight bears. So, as you can see, Pod, they don't mind a challenge. Like you trying to get Virginia to like you. Same thing. Sort of.'

Virginia is a girl from another suburb who

we met at the Sockby Pool. She's very nice and I ring her up and email her all the time. Well, sometimes I do. Well, I don't very often, but I'd like to. It's just that I can never think of anything to say; so our relationship is kind of on hold. Temporarily.

'I think she already likes me a *little* bit,' I say.

Shiny gives the wolverine fangs and some wrap-around sunglasses.

'Well,' he says, 'we could take her and her friend Jodie out on the Sockby Ornamental Lake. Get some practice in before the big voyage. Because if you tip over in the creek, Pod, you're definitely gunna smack your head on a washing machine or a shopping trolley. And as they say, a drowned explorer is a dead explorer. End of story.'

That's true.

'You ring the girls about next Saturday, Poddy.' Shine adds boxing gloves to the wolverine's front paws. 'And I'll make sure the canoe is ship-shape. Deal?'

Er, deal.

Bravely, I ring Virginia and tell her about our canoe, and how Shine and I would like to take her and Jodie, if they're available, for a ride next Saturday on the Sockby Ornamental Lake.

'We'll be there, Pod,' Virginia says. 'I can always rely on you guys for some sort of an adventure.'

I think Virginia's referring to our mini-bike ride along the old railway line, which ended up with our mini-bikes falling off a bridge and disappearing forever.

'Our parents are a lot happier this time,' I say. 'Because there's no petrol or engines involved.'

'And we can bring our own life jackets,' Virginia says. 'Because Jodie's dad's got a speedboat and he has some. I'm really looking forward to it, Pod.'

'So am I,' I mumble. '*Andseeingyou*,' I add at the speed of light. 'I mean, seeing you two at two. Next Saturday. At the Ornamental Lake. Bye.' And I hang up.

Phew–eee!

Man, suddenly it's got *so* hot in here.

By the time I get back to the shed, Shiny has painted the boxing wolverines on the bow, using thirty-year-old marine paint that has been banned from sale in about fifty countries, according to Grandpa Jack.

'It might have a *fraction* of lead in it,' Grandpa Jack says, drinking a beer as he watches us. 'But as long as you don't put it on your sandwiches, she'll be apples. See yers later.' He goes outside, whistling to the tame magpies on the fence.

'Actually, lead's not all that bad.' Shiny adds some silver streaks to the wolverines' fur to give it some nice highlights. 'According to the Sugar Bix Old Histree Fax Pak, the ancient Romans used it for drinking cups, Pod, and they were, like, the smartest people on earth. Even though none of their temples appear to have roofs, which makes you wonder.'

The matching wolverines look fierce and snarly with their boxing gloves, shades and combat helmets, although one wolverine seems to have an extra paw.

'I dunno how that happened,' Shine says. 'Still, it shows that even physically challenged wolverines can also be high achievers, so I say it stays. It'll put us at peace with all our animal brothers, even the ones who aren't exactly ten out of ten.'

I agree. In fact, I like the five-pawed wolverine best; he looks a little bit more like he could come from Sockby, where lots of things are not quite right, and I'm not joking. For example, our school motto is, 'Try harder. We're sick of coming last.'

'Next Saturday,' says Shine, throwing his paintbrush out the window, and into the weeds, 'I reckon we'll impress the girls somethin' *shockin'*.' Shine catches my eye. 'In a good way, Pod, in a good way.'

Chapter 4

I ride my bike to Shiny's house early on Saturday afternoon so that we have plenty of time to take the *Wolverine* down to the Ornamental Lake. My parents are quite happy about the canoe, as they think that carrying it around the streets is all that we will ever do with it.

'I used to have a similar hobby myself, Peter, in my younger, wilder days,' my dad told me at breakfast. 'Often you'd see me out and about on Saturday with a two-metre-tall sunflower in a pot, maximising its sunlight exposure. I made a lot of new friends that way. Gee, the good old days, eh?'

'Ah, yeah,' I'd said. Then, praying that I hadn't inherited one little bit of the infamous Podlewski family gardening madness, I'd bolted.

Shine and I set off carrying the *Wolverine* toward Sockby Ornamental Lake. After a few hundred metres or so, we stop for a rest.

'Boy, this is hard work, bro.' Shine takes a plastic box from his pocket filled with dark squares of . . . something. 'Want a piece of pemmican, Pod? It's great.'

'Pemmi-*what*?' I keep my hands in my pockets. 'I don't do drugs, Shine. No way.'

'Oh, it's not drugs, Pod.' Shiny takes out a piece. 'It's Indian food. It's made from pounded-up dried meat and fat all mixed together. The Sugar Bix Original Recipe Card did suggest adding five teaspoons of sugar, so I added fifteen just to be on the safe side. Go on. Have a bit. It's good. Not too sweet, but just sweet enough.'

So, sitting next to the *Wolverine*, looking down over the Sockby Telephone Pole Exhibit to the Ornamental Lake, I eat some pemmican.

'Hey, this stuff's not too bad,' I say. 'How'd you flatten the meat out? With your mum's rolling pin? And then dry it out in the oven?'

'Nope,' says Shine. 'I did it the traditional way. I used me cricket bat on the footpath and then me sister's hairdryer. I can't quite remember if it was on Hot Style or Blow 'n' Go, but I'll check it out if you want to make some yourself.'

Pass.

At the sight of Virginia and Jodie sitting by the lake, my heart gives a double whammy, because they are the best, friendliest girls we know, and Shiny's just pushed the canoe hard into my chest.

'Hey, girls!' Shiny waves. '*Howdy*! Good to see ya!'

Then we are running towards them, the paddles rattling in the *Wolverine* like applause, and the girls are waving back.

Chapter 5

It's a beautiful sunny afternoon. There are kids everywhere, and stacks of model yachts and ships busily cruising back and forth on Sockby Ornamental Lake.

'You can't use that kayak here,' says a bloke wearing red slippers and holding a black remote control. 'It's against the law.'

'It's not a kayak,' says Shine. 'It's a canoe. They're not even spelt the same.' And with that, all four of us hop into the *Wolverine,* and paddle away.

'Keep an eye out for that dude.' Shine looks

over his shoulder. 'He's got a famous model German battleship called the *Bismarck*, and it could be lurking out behind Little Ducky Island. If it opens fire, hit it with your paddle. Oops!'

We've just run over a model sailing ship, and looking back, it seems to be sinking.

'Oh, dear,' says Virginia. She's wearing sunglasses and sipping orange juice. 'That was Captain Cook's *Endeavour*.'

'Don't worry about it,' Shine says. 'They've got lifeboats. Just keep paddlin', Pod.'

I do, and soon we are in the peace and quiet of the Lois Lowrey Gumboot Lagoon, where Lois Lowrey lost a lot of gumboots, or so the sign says.

'This is lovely, Pod.' Virginia smiles at me. 'I'm so glad you rang us.'

'So am I,' says Shiny, taking a handful of chips from a huge packet in the bottom of the canoe.

'Otherwise we wouldn't hardly have any snacks at all.' He holds up a freak triple-fold chip. 'Thanks for bringin' the junk food, girls. Cheers.'

'That's all right, Shiny.' Jodie dreamily draws a circle in the water with a finger, her long red hair hanging down. 'It's so nice out here. It's perfect.'

'Apart from the smell of animal fat and dried blood from the sheepskins at the tannery,' adds Shine. 'Still. They gotta make ug boots and industrial grease somewhere, and Sockby's just lucky enough to be it. Baaaah!'

We drift around talking about what we've been doing over the eight months since we've seen each other, which in Shiny's case, and mine, is nothing.

'We went on a school trip to France,' Jodie says. 'Didn't we, Virgy? And a girls' surfing camp.'

'Our school doesn't do camps anymore.' Shine

tries to bat a dragonfly out of the air with his paddle. 'Too many kids ended up on the news.'

Virginia smiles, firstly at Shine, and then at me. 'But we've never been in a canoe before, Pod. This is beautiful. That Mr Beanland must be very nice to simply give it to you guys.'

'Oh, yeah, he's cool all right,' says Shine. 'He's also one hell of a Totem Tennis player. A double-handed twin-bat blind-folded freestyler. And they don't come along every day.'

I look around. Willow trees dance a leafy Hula, ducks happily paddle and honk, and all you can hear is kids laughing, and techno music exploding as if someone's speeding through a minefield in a tank.

'Mr B actually made this canoe,' says Shine. 'And because he's from Canada, and such an old pensioner legend, we're going to paddle it down the Sockby Creek to the bay to commemorate the Australian-Canadian war.' Shine digs into his pocket. 'Hey? D'you girls want some pemmican?'

Wisely, they refuse.

'This trip down the creek,' Virginia says. 'How are you going to get the canoe home? You won't be able to paddle all the way back upstream, will you?'

Shine and I look at each other. We hadn't thought about that.

'Well,' Virginia says, 'what about me and Jode meet you at Williamstown jetty? It's pretty close to where the Yarra runs into the bay. And we can help you get it home on the train.'

'Excellent,' says Shine promptly. 'That'll be a piece of cake. I bet stacks of people take boats around on public transport every day. D'you have a mobile for communication purposes?'

'I do.' Virginia takes out a fantastic-looking mobile phone. 'I got it for my birthday.'

'Boy,' says Shine. 'Is that an SB 500? You must've eaten a *power* of Sugar Bix to get the Frequent Muncha Points for that. But, hey, check this out.' Shiny takes out *his* phone, which is shaped like a dog bone. 'It's a genuine Dog and Bone Phone from the good people at Brekky Cola, the wake-up cola suitable for adults, infants, and your canine companion. Man, you should hear the ring tone.'

'It's a blue heeler barking at a ute doing a burn-out,' I add.

'You are *so* right.' Shine's face glows with pride. 'It's worth a fortune.'

'So we'll *see* you at the sea.' Jodie shoots out a hand, catches the dragonfly Shine was trying to stun, then releases it unharmed. 'It's a bit of a pity we can't come paddling, but that's okay. We'll be the token chicks meeting you at the other end.'

'Right on!' says Shine.

'You girls aren't token chicks,' I add quickly.

'I bet if there was any trouble you'd help us out big time.'

'Right on, again!' Shine high-fives the back of my head. 'You can *always* rely on us for trouble, can't you, Pod? There's never been a shortage of that when we're around, no worries!'

Unfortunately, he's right about that.

Chapter 6

Whenever Shiny tells me something is simple, I worry. And whenever he tells me he's got everything organised, I get ready to hit the panic button.

'Next Saturday going down the creek will run like clockwork, Pod,' Shine says, 'because I've already sorted out our parents.' He wipes mud off the *Wolverine's* side with a rag.

'Really?' I find it hard to believe Shiny has come up with anything that will give us all Saturday to paddle down to the bay without our folks interfering. 'What'd you tell them?'

'First,' Shiny says, 'I told 'em there's a Canadian Canoe Safety Demonstration at the lake followed by a three-hour, fully supervised paper hat-making workshop, which is then topped off with the Moonlight Blue Light Paddling, Tadpoling, and Boogie Disco. I've already printed off the flyers. It should be great. There's a police presence, compulsory fruit consumption, a courtesy canoe bus, and everyone home by ten. And only five dollars to get in.'

'They'll never believe it,' I say.

'They already do,' Shine says. 'And my folks are taking *your* folks to catch the Early Bird Gets The Worm dinner special at the Sockby Pokie Lounge, and then on to see the new Lawrence Lame movie at the Sockby BYO Cinema and Driving Range. It's locked in. And so simple it might even work.'

Once again I am amazed at the way Shine's

mind works, his guts and determination. And just how dumb our parents actually are.

'But we've got be home by ten,' Shiny says. 'Or my folks said they'll remove every last one of the new beans they put in my beanbag. So. You know they mean business. They've done it before.'

'You're joking?' I say. 'They sorted out all the old beans from all the new beans in your beanbag and took them away?'

Shiny nods. 'Yep. Hid 'em on top of the wardrobe, and only let me have 'em back six at a time. It was a tough couple of years, Poddy, a tough couple of years.'

I think it would be true to say that the Diamonds are an *interesting* family.

Chapter 7

The week goes by with me making many phone-calls to Shiny and Virginia so that everyone knows exactly what's going on with Saturday's *Sockby to the Sea* expedition.

'I emailed you a map,' Virginia tells me. 'It's got the whole route marked, and where we're going to meet. It's quite a long way, Pod. And there are some dangerous-looking spots. There are even some rapids. And, er, ships at the end. You'll have to watch out.'

'We'll be fine,' I say. 'I mean, truly, I got a badge

at Cubs for Carrying A Full Cup Of Tea Very Carefully, and Shiny has a Sugar Bix First Aid Kit loaded with chocolate-coated medical supplies. So, no worries.'

'Yeah,' says Virginia, doubtfully. 'No worries at all.'

'Anyway,' I add. 'See you on Saturday at Williamstown before the sun goes down. For the big celebration. There'll probably be fireworks.'

'There probably will be, Pod.' Virginia laughs. 'Of one sort or another.'

I'm not sure what she means by that, so I just say goodbye, and hang up. I then spend a minute thinking about tackling the Sockby Creek, the mighty Yarra River, and whatever lies beyond. I also notice that it's started to rain, which will certainly make the paddling easier. Or that's the theory, anyway.

As I print out the map, I think about what a

great girl Virginia is. She's lived in America, she now lives in a posh suburb that even has hills, and she goes to a flashy rich-chicks-only school, yet she's *always* interested in what Shine and I set out to do. She's also gorgeous, funny, smart and gutsy, and she keeps it real. She's the perfect girl. And you don't meet them every day.

Or I don't.

The rain has stopped. It's now hailing. The sound of it on the roof is like fifty tonnes of frozen peas dumped from a jumbo jet. This won't please my dad, as it will damage his plants; but like many things that can't be stopped by complaining – you just have to ride them out to the end.

Like the good old Sockby Creek!

And the mighty, murky, muddy Yarra River.

Chapter 8

I get to Shine's place early on Saturday morning to escape any Podlewski gardening activities, such as today's micro search of the lawn for Bindi-Eye, which are tiny, spiky weeds that my dad says were introduced to Australia by the Mafia to overthrow the government, and are responsible for puncturing many thousands of bicycle tyres.

Shiny answers the door carrying a Sugar Bix box and a bowl of cereal that glitters.

'Check these Sugar Bix Stax of Wild West Facts, Poddy.' He shows me the box. 'It says that beavers wouldn't be nearly as busy as they are if they didn't build their dams in the water. And that those old wild west 'coonskin caps were actually made from the skin of a *dead* raccoon, and not a tame live one just sitting on your head.'

'That's amazing, Shine,' I say. 'Why don't you skip that cereal for once and have an apple? Then we can get down to the creek straightaway.'

'Good thinkin'.' Shine takes out something on a stick from his pocket. 'I just happen to have a Sugar Bix Healthy Teeth Toffee Apple right here.'

'Where are your parents?' I look down the Diamonds' hallway, and see a black-and-white guinea pig run from one room to another. 'Have they gone out?'

Shine nods. 'Yeah, Grandpa heard about a ripper 1964 Holden that's been under a tarp under a pine tree for thirty years. So it'll be, like, in mint condition. They all took off early in case anyone beats them to it.'

'But that's *older* than his old car was,' I say. 'Why doesn't he get a newer one?'

'Oh, he never drives now.' Shine cracks his toffee apple against the door frame. 'So it hardly matters. Anyway, scary shirt, Poddy. Man, it's, like, electric. Purple, white *and* yellow. Whoo. *Nasty*.'

My mum insisted I wear it for the Moonlight Blue Light Disco that's never going to happen. Shine blinks rapidly.

'We'll have to cover it up, Poddy. I can't be lookin' at that all day. I'll go blind.'

That makes two of us.

We load the *Wolverine* with food and water, a length of rope, Shiny's disposable camera, Virginia's map, and a spare paddle. In the morning sunlight the canoe shines. I look at it and hope Mr Beanland will be happy back in Canada.

'I bet Mr B wishes he could come with us,' I say. 'He's a brave guy. He flew bombers in the war. And once, his plane was shot down by a squadron of Messerschmitt fighters. He had to bail out over Germany and was taken prisoner.'

'Yeah, well, accidents do happen,' says Shine. He looks at me. 'As you and I well know, Pod.'

Well, yes, Shiny and I have had a few bike, tandem bike, unicycle, mini-bike, kite, model aeroplane, scooter, roller blade, skateboard, wheelbarrow, billycart, and homemade sub-marine accidents.

Shine looks out the grimy shed windows.

'I feel lucky, Poddy. We've had just the right amount of rain to get the old Sockby Creek flowing, but not absolutely raging, because canoeing in a flash flood won't get you far.'

Shiny thinks about that. 'Well, it will, but it might be upside-down.'

'And we don't want to do that, do we, Shine?' I say.

'Nope. Check these out. Grandpa Jack borrowed 'em.'

Shiny picks up two orange life jackets. 'The bloke actually couldn't quite remember Grandpa, so there's no chance he'll be comin' around to take them back any time soon. And look, they've got Police Rescue printed on the back. Cool, eh? And here. Wear this over that freaked-out fright-night shirt.'

Shine takes Grandpa Jack's old duck-hunting coat down from a hook. It has pictures of dead ducks all over it as camouflage. I put it on, take some shotgun shells out of the pocket, and hide them on a high shelf.

'You shoulda seen the pants mum got for me,'

I tell Shine. 'They had tartan patch pockets with matching squares on the knees. I could've got a job as a scarecrow.'

Shiny nods thoughtfully. 'Well, you do have the build for it, Pod. Kind of like a bunch of sticks, and long. The Wizard of Oz style, they're calling it. I mean, chicks are over the six-pack thing. Skinny is in. I deadset read that in the Sugar Bix Style File For Young Folks.'

'Time to get to that creek,' I say, for about a million reasons, most of them personal.

So we set off towards the Sockby Creek carrying the mighty *Wolverine*.

'It's a pity the Canoe Orientation Day and Moonlight Blue Light Disco got canned,' Shiny says, as we carry the *Wolverine* between the closed-down dog soap factory and the closed-down cowboy hat factory. 'Because there's not much on these days to keep us Sockby kids off the streets, and away from the creeks and drains, where we might hurt ourselves.'

'But Shine,' I say, 'it never really was on, was it?' Man, this canoe is getting heavy. 'It was all just a trick you made up to fool our parents.'

'Yeah, I know.' Shiny puts a big piece of pemmican into his mouth. 'But still. I went to a lot of effort to set it up just to see it knocked on the head at the last moment. It's very disappointing.'

As much as I think Shine's a super smart guy, I sometimes do wonder what sort of a job he's going to get.

Chapter 9

The creek doesn't flow very fast as Sockby is flat, plus the Sockby Flood Retarding Basin holds back most of the water, fence posts, wheelie bins, rubbish bags, and polystyrene that make the Sockby Creek the thing of beauty that it is today – or so the council brochure says. Still, it swirls and whirls, the colour of clay.

Shine hands me a paddle, eyes narrowed as he judges the power of the creek. 'Just like the Amazon, Poddy. Except somewhat smaller.' He tightens his life jacket. 'Let's rock!' He holds up a fist. 'Let's do this for Mr Beanland, the unofficial world champion of Totem Tennis, the unofficial international head of the entire rubber band industry, and the unofficial patron saint of canoe exploration. Amen.'

'Amen,' I say, although I don't know why. 'I'll hold it steady while you get in.'

Shiny clambers into the *Wolverine* from the rubbishy bank and gets settled in front. Then I hop in and we're away, the *Wolverine* wobbling wildly but soon steadying as she meets the current like a long-lost friend.

'Bon voyage to us!' Shine's voice arrows across the flat, thistle-spiked paddocks of the Sockby Industrial Estate. 'Next stop, the *open* sea!'

Not quite. We've just rammed into a huge soggy cardboard box full of what looks like dumped hospital sheets and pillows.

'Back up, Pod!' Shine paddles madly in reverse.

'There's a bedpan here just like Grandpa Jack's. And that's not somethin' you want to fool around with.'

I paddle backwards, we dodge the box, then we're on our way again, the creek winding around a stooping gum tree that a jolly swagman might've camped under. It feels like we're gliding through the world, the quietness of the old factories soothing and calm.

'Make sure you use the J-stroke, Pod.' Shiny demonstrates this in the caramel-coloured water. 'Because that single stroke is the basis of all good canoeing, according to champion Sugar Bix Can-Do Canoeing Coach, Brian P. Toggle, who won gold at the 1948 Olympics. It was in the long jump. But still, he was one hell of a canoeist.'

Oh, boy. Sometimes there's not a lot I can say to Shine.

In a way, we're travelling through Sockby's

history. There are dumped vintage cars, old couches, fridges, and signs on silent factories for products that no longer exist. And there's me and Shine, on the look-out for the ghosts of Sockby, who spend their years hoping for better times, which probably won't ever arrive.

'She just slides along, the old *Wolverine*, doesn't she?' says Shine, as we steer around blocks of concrete so big they must've been carried here by another civilisation. 'Like time itself, the current beneath our keel moving us on towards the distant coasts of life. Onward, Peter, ever onward.'

Where the *hell* did that come from?

'Yikes!' yells Shine. 'Look out, Pod! There's a dead cat here the size of a flamin' lion! Oh, no it's not. It's a shagpile toilet floor mat with a smiley face pattern. Man, *that's* a relief. We used to have one just like it. Except ours was a little bit more yellowish.'

We paddle on, me thinking about Virginia and Jodie, and how we're all going to meet up at Williamstown to celebrate our epic voyage.

'You know Virginia and Jodie?' I say. 'One day we should go out on a real date with them. Like, to the movies, or to tea. Since they're the best girls that we've ever known.'

Shine paddles thoughtfully. 'Yeah. For sure. Perhaps we could get them along to the Centenary Exhibition of One Hundred Years of Professional Wrestling in Australia? There's old wrestling tights and everything. You can even buy the capes. I bet they'd love that.'

'I, er, bet they would,' I say. 'Hey, how good is this?'

The creek has slowed and flows out into a wide marshy lake surrounded by head-high reeds and healthy-looking trees. Suddenly Sockby seems a long way away, and as we paddle along, I can actually hear a frog, although it might just be a novelty horn beeping out on the highway. No, it's a frog.

I look around. 'It even smells good, Shine. Like real *dirty* dirt and real *watery* water. We've actually discovered something. I never knew this was here.'

'Neither did I.' Shine glances at a small group of trees that look to be sneaking up on the lake, as if they can't believe it's here, either. 'You see, Poddy? Disobeyin' your parents *is* educational.' Shiny looks up at a tiny bird that hovers and twitters like a melodic maniac. 'And that noisy little ratbag is known as a meadow lark because –'

'You've got the Sugar Bix Birdwatchers Companion,' I say. 'I saw it next to your mum's Sugar Bix Extra Short Bible for Extra Busy People.'

'That's right, bro.' Shine paddles confidently on.

'The whole family's into it, Pod. We're livin' the Sugar Bix lifestyle. It gives you the perfect work-life-school balance.'

'But what about your dad, Shine?' I ask. 'He hasn't got a job.'

Shine flicks a clump of brown weed off his paddle. At least, I hope it's weed.

'Yeah, but me mum's got three. So that's where the balance comes in. Now, Poddy, it's time to point the old *Wolverine* down Sockby Creek, to where we'll meet the dangerous and dirty waters of the hellish Yarra River.'

'I'll check the map.' I stash my paddle, and take the map out of my backpack. 'Right. Now the Sockby Creek splits into two about a kilometre away, and I think the safest way to go is –'

A sudden gust of wind snatches the map and flings it high over the wall of reeds. And it's gone, just like that.

'Don't worry about it,' says Shine. 'Maps are too hard to read anyway. All those stupid squiggly little lines, and north's always the same on every map, which can't be right. Let's just get goin' and hope for the best. As usual.'

We do, and twenty seconds later almost get swept into the wide-open mouth of a flooded quarry.

'Power *on*, Poddy!' Shine yells, as the *Wolverine* scrapes along a black nest of cables that look like a family of Loch Ness monsters fighting over the remote control. 'If we get caught in there, we'll drown like rats!'

We paddle hard, digging deep into the dark water, the *Wolverine* rasping her way free. Then we are out into the main stream of the current, cruising along, a flight of ducks honking good wishes as they fly past. Something wet and white splashes into the water close beside me.

'That dirty duck nearly *pooped* on me!' I say. 'Another metre and I would've got it right in the eye. I could've been blinded!'

Shiny rests, paddle across his knees.

'They saw your jacket, Pod. They've got long memories, ducks. Like elephants. And they're smarter than homing pigeons, too. Except they don't have homes to go to. Or not what a pigeon would call a home. So they're a little stuck with that piece of the puzzle.'

I take two vanilla slices from my lunchbox and hand one to Shine. Hopefully that might give him time to think about what he just said, and not say any more.

'Oh, *man*, Pod!' Shine takes a big bite. 'These things are *awesome*. Did you know that the Sockby Ye Old Pie Shop has competed in the Vanilla Slice of the Year contest for the last fifty years, and has only come last sixteen times?'

'No, but it doesn't surprise me,' I say. 'Anyway, let's paddle. The creek forks soon, where there's some rapids. And then it meets up with the Yarra River, I think. According to the map we used to have.'

'Forget the rapids, Pod!' Shiny grabs his paddle. 'Waterfall ahead! Go left! Go *left*! Go *LEFT*!'

Chapter 10

The waterfall isn't really a waterfall, it's an outfall pipe spewing bright green liquid from a factory that *is* operating, and operating full-speed ahead. A flying torrent smashes into the Sockby Creek from five metres up. If we go under that, we'll sink in two seconds flat.

'Hard left!' Shine digs in on the right side of the canoe while I use my paddle as a rudder to turn us as quickly as possible. 'That's great, Poddy! We're gunna make it!'

There are waves going in all directions. The

air is hazy with pale green mist and spray. And through it all the *Wolverine* bucks and rocks, water crashing on board, but not enough to sink or stop us. We've made it!

'*Pshwah!*' Shiny spits, shaking his wet head. 'That tastes like my mum's chicken soup!'

It does a bit, but there's no time to worry about that.

'Look out for the backwash, Shine!' I yell. 'We gotta meet it bow-first! Or we'll tip!'

Waves come at us side-on, bouncing off a concrete wall where another drain pours into the creek.

Shiny turns, water coursing down his cheeks. 'Which end is the bow again, Pod? Because if we were heading backwards upstream, it'd be different, wouldn't it? And I get confused because –'

'*Your* end!' I shout. 'Paddle harder on the right!'

We paddle like madmen, the *Wolverine* meeting the waves, slicing through them. And once again we roller-coaster our way through danger, and on down the Sockby Creek, witnessed only by a bloke taking his three attack dogs for a walk.

'Nice goin', boys!' he calls out. 'But look out for the whirlpools that are just near the *big* –'

At that moment the dogs go mad and I miss the last bit.

'Just near the big *what*?' I ask Shine. 'Did you get that?'

'Well, it wouldn't be near the Big Prawn.' Shine shakes his head. 'Because that's like five thousand K away. Or the Big Apple, because that's in New York. And it wouldn't be the Big Bosoms, because they're still on the drawing board –'

'Forget it, Shine,' I say. 'I'm sure we'll find out whatever it is pretty soon.'

Shiny nods. 'Like the results from those

scholarship exams we did. D'you reckon we'll get one, Poddy?'

'Er, no,' I say. 'Not unless someone made a really serious mistake.'

Chapter 11

We paddle along a quiet stretch of the creek, kept company by a school of purple ice-cream containers. I try to ignore the new houses, the footy grounds, the toilet block, and imagine that we're out in the wilderness. Then, suddenly, I reckon I can see the *big* thing that guy was talking about.

'Man, scope that bridge,' says Shine. 'It is giganti-mega-*normulous*.'

The bridge stands about twenty metres high on huge concrete supports, and carries six lanes of cars from one side of the valley to the other. The creek flows beneath it into cold shadow, where two huge drains pour water into a man-made pool that looks deep, dirty, and treacherous.

'I can't see any whirlpools,' Shine says. 'Let's just go for it. I mean, what could a whirlpool possibly do to a full-sized canoe? Did you ever see *Titanic*, Pod? Boy, that was a grouse movie. And they didn't worry about whirlpools, did they?'

I stop the canoe by paddling backwards. 'Let's look before we leap, Shine. It's better to be safe than sorry, as my mum says. You know, patience is a virtue.' There. That should slow him down for a minute, at least.

'He who hesitates is *lost*!' Shiny starts paddling like a wind-up monkey, the *Wolverine* heading off downstream. '*Always* stand under a tree to avoid lightning! And *never* swim until you've eaten a really *huge* lunch!'

Shiny has the current on his side. There's nothing I can do to stop the canoe, and in seconds we're under the bridge, where drains unload tonnes of water, a series of whirlpools spinning like tornado-flavoured milkshakes.

'Yee ha!' Shiny yells as the *Wolverine* skids sideways. 'Go baby!' Shiny spits into the centre of a whirlpool. 'Give us what you got, creek! *Ramp* it up! *Bring* it on!' We wobble and sway through water that slides curling, grasping fingers along the canoe's sides. Suddenly Shine lurches sideways. 'Prepare to abandon ship, Pod! We're goin' down!'

The *Wolverine* dives into the middle of a whirlpool, but her curved bow refuses to go under, and then we are out in the sunshine, Shine waving his paddle like a victory flag.

'You see, Poddy! Explorers don't *have* to think. They just go for it. How do you reckon they discovered what head hunters do? Or how people make jungle pits full of spikes? Not by asking, or thinking about it, that's for sure. They just bowled right on in. Too easy!'

'Hey, speaking of explorers, Shine,' I say. 'Whatever did happen to great, great, grand-Uncle Trevor after the Burke and Wills . . . expedition.' I was going to call it a disaster, but Shiny might have taken offence.

He shrugs, paddling smoothly.

'That's the funny thing, Pod. Grand-Uncle Trev went off to sell cooking pots to these friendly cannibal tribes, and never came back. Years later, his diary was found. Full of weird recipes, it was. None of them vegetarian. Although there was one final note that said everything tasted like chicken. It was probably rabbit, though, I reckon.'

There's not a lot I can add to that – so I don't. Instead, I keep a sharp look-out for navigational hazards. Dead ahead, the creek forks, falling away in two streams that shoot over rocky rapids then disappear between tall, grassy banks.

'Which way, Poddy?' Shiny paddles backwards, keeping the canoe still. 'Right or left? Flip a coin or what?'

From memory, the right-hand fork looked *longer* on the map, so in theory it should be *less* steep, and not as fast-flowing.

'Go left,' I say.

'Right!' says Shiny.

'No, freakin' *left*!' I yell.

'Right!'

'Oh, whatever,' I mutter, as the *Wolverine* makes its own mind up, and veers straight towards thirty metres of jagged rocks, sheets of leaping spray, and a deadly tangle of shopping trolleys. 'Hold onto your hat, Shine! We're goin' in!'

And in we go.

Chapter 12

The *Wolverine* leaps into the rapids and bangs off a slimy black log before sliding down a chute of water that is smooth and clear – apart from a low branch that will knock our heads off if we don't duck.

'Look out!' I yell, as the canoe slides beneath it. 'Duck!'

Shiny springs up, paddling hard to avoid the jagged jaws of a rusty steel barrel.

'Compression!' he shouts. 'Dead ahead, Pod! Paddle left! I mean, *on* the right!'

I do what Shiny says, even though I don't know what a *compression* is – then we are weaving fast around upside-down shopping trolleys and toothy-looking rocks. The *Wolverine*, caught up in the rush of the water, scrapes over an old suitcase, skids around someone's dumped letterbox, then shoots out through seething brown froth onto a slow river that's forty metres wide and looks deep.

'That was *so* cool!' I say, my heart thumping. 'We did that *really* well.'

'Yer damn straight,' says Shine. 'That was definitely a Sugar Bix Maxi Moment that deserves a Sugar Bix Super Dooper Sucrose High Kilojoule Reward. Here, Pod. Munch on this.' Shine tosses me something that looks like a Rubik's Cube made from crushed lollies and broken glass. 'There. That'll challenge your back teeth.'

Only if I eat it.

The river bank rises toward three-storey houses

that hide among old trees. It's as if we're in a private valley, away from the worries of the world, and the dull streets and dead factories of Sockby.

'Oh, man,' Shiny says, looking around. 'This is *so* nice. Look, that place's even got its own wine farm.'

Shiny's right, in a way; there is a little vineyard, the grape vines hanging from wires in straight, beautiful rows, their leaves red, gold and yellow. And there are houses with private jetties, wooden boatsheds, and gardens with white chairs and tables where you could sit for hours, just watching the river go by. It seems impossible that Sockby is even in the same *state*.

'Big city dead-ahead, Poddy,' says Shine, as we drift around a long bend. 'We're closin' in.'

Ahead, like giants getting to their feet, silver-grey buildings stand tall over the soft green tops of trees. Seeing them, I *do* feel like an explorer, or an adventurer – I feel *braver*, anyway. Quietly, I slip my Sugar Bix Cube-thing into the river, thinking that I've got all the reward I need without adding half a kilogram of sugar. Sorry, fish.

The river straightens. There are bike paths and little bridges along its reedy edges, and a freeway curves past, cars flashing by. But I really like this slow paddling. It gives me a chance to see things I've never seen before.

'We should've brought some beads and tomahawks to trade with the locals,' Shine says. 'That footy ground over there'd be a good bet.' Shine points to a massive concrete stadium about fifteen storeys high. 'You know, Pod, once great, great, grand-Uncle Trev swapped his last pair of pants for a stuffed hippopotamus, but its tail fell off, so he had to leave it in Africa. Pity. It'd be worth a fortune these days. That's a true story, Pod. A true story.'

# Chapter 13

We're in the middle of the city, and it's amazing. There are thin wooden racing boats like insects, with oars for legs, and clumsy sight-seeing ferries that remind me of caravans caught in a flood. Occasionally, a little old-fashioned steamboat toodles by. One toots at us with its whistle.

'Grand-Uncle Trevor had one of them a hundred years ago.' Shine watches the tubby timber boat chug off, brass portholes shining. 'He put wheels on it, but unfortunately wrote it off in the Simpson Desert. Evidently he was trying to avoid someone's cat. The good news, Pod, is that no one got hurt. Yes, you can fix a car-boat. But cats are more difficult. Especially if they're dead.'

Shine is a very imaginative boy, that's all I can say.

Around us, buildings take up most of the sky, and people by their hundreds sit in cafes lined up along the bank. I think of Virginia and Jodie, and hope they've made it to Williamstown, which should only be a few hundred metres across the bay from the mouth of the river.

'Be seeing the girls soon,' I say, tired now, my arms and shoulders aching. 'We're in the home straight, Shine.'

'Mr Beanland would be proud.' Shine nods with satisfaction. 'We've taken the canoe out twice and haven't sunk it once. Look *out*, Pod! There's a rubbish catcher dead ah – damn!'

We've paddled straight into a big plastic boom-thing that's filled with millions of disposable coffee cups, plastic bottles, sticks, tennis balls, plastic dolls, and a blow-up whale. People on shore start to laugh and clap.

'I bet this never happened to great, great, grand-Uncle Trevor,' I mutter, blushing as we do our best to back out of twenty square metres of rubbish.

'Funny you should say that, Poddy.' Shiny flips a red football sock off his paddle. 'Because Uncle Trev *did* get bogged in a tip. Apparently Burke and Wills sent him down to dump some junk after their garage sale flopped, and his wagon got caught in a hole full of convict ladies' old undies.'

Why do I find that so hard to believe?

The sound of the city is amazing, like an orchestra tuning up but never playing; noise coming from cars, trucks, trams, trains, boats, helicopters, people, cafes, and from the river itself, which makes a million little splashes and slaps.

Now it's widening. And the boats using it are getting bigger and bigger.

'Better stay out to the left,' Shine says. 'And keep out of everybody's way. These fishing guys mean business.'

A steel fishing trawler comes up the middle of the river, pushing out a bow wave like a bouncer charging through a crowd. The crew don't even look sideways, and suddenly the *Wolverine* seems out of place, riding unsteadily, her timber sides like eggshells compared to the hulls of all these other larger boats.

'Do you get the feeling, Poddy,' Shiny asks, 'that maybe we've paddled into the *wrong* neighbourhood?' He looks around at the widening river, the warehouses, building sites, and concrete wharfs. 'And maybe it's only gunna get wronger?'

'We'll be cool,' I say, not very confidently. 'If we're careful. You can swim, can't you?' I mean this as a joke; in summer Shine and I spend so many weeks at our local pool that our boardies fade to grey and our ears never need cleaning.

'Well, sometimes I forget really important things in an emergency,' Shine says. 'Once Grandpa Jack got stuck on the toilet, and I forgot where the crowbar was. *Then* I rang 911 instead of 000, and got an American lady who wanted to send in the US Special Forces and a spy camera.'

'What happened in the end?' I ask. Ahead, beyond a huge bridge, I can see the bay; it's dark blue, which in my book of seamanship means it's probably over my head, and deep enough to support a shark the size of a nuclear submarine.

Shine paddles on the left, to keep the *Wolverine's*

bow heading into the choppy waves that have sprung up in the wind.

'Well, Pod, luckily some very nice religious ladies turned up at the front door. But before they freed Gramps, they poked their brochures under the toilet door, and made him read 'em all out loud. He learnt a lot. It worked out fine.'

There's never a dull moment at the Diamonds' house; whereas at my house, the gardening and composting centre of Sockby, it's dull every minute of the year – although I'm starting to wish things were a bit duller around *here*, because I can now see those huge red cranes that unload container ships, meaning there must be ships not too far away.

Meanwhile, we paddle under a bridge so tall and so wide it hides the sky.

'I don't get why they'd build this thing *so* tall.' Shine looks up. 'Surely ships can't be *that* big?'

The bridge must be almost a hundred metres above the water.

'I hope not,' I say. 'Because this channel is where they go. Which we have to cross to get to Williamstown.'

'Uncle Trevor tried to swim the English Channel once,' Shine says. 'But he got so exhausted three-quarters of the way across, he had to turn around, and swim all the way back. He was devastated.'

'If that's Williamstown over there,' Shine says, as we come out from under the bridge, 'we haven't got too far to go.'

Perhaps a kilometre ahead, across the channel, are low buildings, and the masts of hundreds of yachts.

'Nope. Not too far.' I look ahead. 'All we've got to do is get across, and we'll be home, safe and sound. No sweat.'

Shine begins to paddle and so do I. The water looks deep. Very deep.

Now I *really* start to look for ships.

Chapter 14

We're on open water now, but thankfully the waves are not big, and the wind has died down. There are no ships coming in or going out, but I can see some tied up – massive things a million times bigger than the *Wolverine*. Behind us is the city, like a picture on a postcard, the buildings cutting a jigsaw shape into the blue sky.

'I'm gunna take a few photos.' Shine takes his disposable camera from his backpack. 'And Poddy, you should ring the girls to see how they're gettin' on. And to tell them that we haven't been sea-assaulted by a whale or squidnapped.'

'Good idea.' I keep paddling, without strength, my hands blistered, my shoulders tightened by bolts of pain. 'We *could* turn back,' I say suddenly, the fear I've been feeling rushing out. 'Before we get right out into the channel. Canoes aren't really made for the sea.'

'We already *are* in the channel.' Shiny takes photographs of the city, the docks, me, the *Wolverine*, and a few of himself. He then takes out his Dog and Bone phone. 'We'll be right, Poddy. Just think of good old Uncle Trevor and the cooking pots. You just ring the girls and tell 'em we'll see 'em in half an hour. No drama.'

I stop paddling and ring Virginia.

'There's been a change of plan, Pod,' Virginia informs me, her voice so clear I'm certain I should be able to see her on the shore. 'Jodie's dad brought his boat down to do some fishing.

So we might come on out and meet you.'

Relief! Instantly my fear evaporates. Or most of it does. We're *safe!* I press the phone to my life jacket.

'Shine! They're coming out to meet us in Jodie's dad's speedboat. So it's plain sailing all the way to Willy! *All* right!' I put the phone back up to my ear. 'That's great, Virginia. We'll see you soon.'

'Okay, Pod. We'll come out just as soon as that big ship's gone through.'

Ship? What ship?

THAT SHIP.

A huge container ship has come out of a dock that was hidden behind another dock. Its black bow is so high and wide it looks like it will barely fit under the bridge. And it carries two monstrous iron anchors that must weigh ten tonnes each.

'Virginia,' I say. 'I'll get back to you, okay? It's

just that we happen to be right in front of that ship, so I'd better go.'

'Oh, Pod.' There's a short silence before Virginia yells. *'Paddle!'*

'Now, Shine,' I add, handing his phone back, 'I don't want you to panic, but look to your right. Starboard, I mean.'

Shine looks to the right, his face goes white, and then his mouth opens.

'SHIIIIIIIP!' His eyes seem to be stuck open. 'We're *gunna* die!'

I feel calm, which is surprising, as my mother always tells anybody who will ever listen that I'm a highly strung, nervy, dithery, chooky, scatter-brained type of kid. 'Not if we start paddling like crazy, we won't. And keep it up until our arms fall off.'

'MOOOOOOOOOOOOOOOOOOOP!'

The ship's horn is so loud it arrives like a gust

of wind, and actually flattens the waves. There's no room for anything else but the sound of that horn, the echo coming back as if it's bounced off the entire city.

Shine's eyes open even wider. He looks like some sort of South American jungle bat. 'Anyway, now that you mention it, Poddy, I think we'd better . . . *PADDLE!*'

Chapter 15

We paddle as hard as we can, the *Wolverine* slicing through the small, choppy waves – but compared to the ship, it's as if we're not moving at all. Its flared black bow, ten storeys high, smashes through the water, hurling out a wave as tall as a door.

'Oh my God,' mutters Shiny. 'I'm not so sure dog-paddle will get me out of this.'

The ship looms, seeming to get bigger and bigger, hunching its shoulders, gathering speed as it prepares for its battle with the open ocean. And we are nothing but a toothpick in its way.

'MOOOOOOOOOOOOOOOOOOOOOP!'

'Do you think he's seen us?' Shine shouts.

'I think so, Shine!' I shout back. 'But he can't stop. So *paddle*!'

My body is fiery with pain as I paddle as hard and fast as I can. The shore looks so far away and the *Wolverine* seems so slow and fragile. And over and above everything is the ship, the sound of her engines a deep churning hum. And then there is her horn.

'MOOOOOOOOOOOOOOOOOOOOP!'

'*Go*, Shine!' I yell. '*Go!*'

'*Go*, Pod!' Shine yells. '*Go!*'

We're no longer in front of the ship, although it is now only about a hundred metres away. At this rate I figure we might not get run down, but simply swamped by the bow wave, dragged along its side, then sucked through the propeller. And I can say that I don't fancy that.

'MOOOOOOOOOOOOOOOOOOOOOP!'

The ship's horn rules the world. It is the loudest sound I've ever heard.

'Oh, gimme a break,' says Shine. '*Please.*'

Ahead, a yellow and white speedboat comes racing towards us, bouncing confidently through the waves, bow up, as if it's a dog searching through long grass for two rabbits – two rabbits called Pod and Shine, I hope.

It *must* be Jodie's dad and the girls.

'There's Jodie's boat, Shine!' I yell. 'Keep paddling! Don't stop!'

I look at the ship. Waves slide helplessly down its side to where the propeller smashes them into foam. Then I see that the speedboat has veered away. It's leaving us behind. Oh no! We're gunna be crushed then smashed then shredded!

'Keep paddlin', Poddy!' Shiny yells. 'When the

going gets tough, the tough rely on a Sugar Bix Quick Fix. So d'you want a – hey, they're coming back!'

The speedboat has done a U-turn and is skimming towards us, skittering over the waves as if it doesn't have a care in the world. Unlike Shiny and me.

'YEAH!' Shiny yells, and drops his paddle. 'I've got the rope!' He holds it up. 'They can tow us in! We're gunna live, Pod! We're gunna save the Wolverine!'

The ship is only fifty metres away, neither turning nor slowing, which it couldn't do in less than half an hour anyway, so I doubt the captain's even bothering to try.

'MOOOOOOOOOOOOOOOOOOOOOOOOP!'

I look at the racing bow waves, the monstrous black hull, and those two anchors that are like enormous knuckledusters.

'Or we could just get into the speedboat, Shine,' I say. 'And get the hell outta here.'

The speedboat pulls up alongside, the girls on board, Jodie's dad at the wheel.

'Get in, boys!' he yells. 'The girls'll help! Move! *Now*! It's too dangerous to tow the canoe!'

I look at Shine and Shine looks at me. We both nod.

'You first, Shine,' I say. 'Then hold the canoe steady for me.'

We paddle to the speedboat and pass our backpacks over. Then Shiny scrambles on board, turning to hold the *Wolverine* while Jodie and Virginia help me get out. Everything seems to be going in different directions, but I make it across, smacking my knee so hard I know I'll be limping for a week.

'Siddown and hold on!' Jodie's dad shouts. 'We're off!'

The twin outboard motors yowl. We take off as if shot from a gun.

'Boy,' says Shine, slumping like a wet sack, 'these seats are nice. Are they leather or vinyl, Jode?'

Behind us the *Wolverine* bobs in the waves, abandoned. I feel terrible. I watch it drifting, falling back, like a friend we've left to die.

'If we'd tried to tow you and the canoe had tipped,' Jodie says, 'we would've all been in trouble. It's bad news, I know, but my dad said this was the safest way.'

That's true, but I can hardly watch as the ship draws level with the *Wolverine*, the bow wave flipping it up then swamping it. But the *Wolverine* doesn't sink.

'It might not get sucked into the propeller,' Shiny says. 'It won't drift full of water like that. It might just stay where it is.'

'It might,' I say, as the ship slides by, the

Wolverine just metres away from it, wallowing, like a little wounded whale. 'We'll soon see.'

Jodie's dad slows the speedboat.

'Here goes,' Shine mumbles. 'Good luck, little *Woolly*. Good luck.'

I'd swear the *Wolverine* is going to be drawn into the thrashing propeller – but, like an exhausted swimmer, it stays afloat, and the ship passes by.

We cheer!

Chapter 16

We've towed the *Wolverine* into shore, and while Jodie's dad, Steve, loads his boat back onto its trailer, the four of us rest. I feel sore all over, exhausted, totally shell-shocked by this afternoon's action. The ship has already gone, a hundred thousand tonnes disappeared into thin air.

'Well, Poddy,' says Shine, 'I think we'd better bring down the Permanent Cone of Silence on today's little adventure, and get on that train as soon as possible. Because if we're late, my mum'll freak out thinkin' that I've hurt myself dancing at the Moonlight Disco.'

I'm not looking forward to carrying the canoe on the train, even if the station isn't far away. I am so tired I could sleep right where I am.

'My dad will take the canoe home for you,' Jodie says. 'But he said it's up to you guys to tell your folks what happened.'

'Too easy.' Shine folds his life jacket and tosses it into the *Wolverine*. 'Honesty's the best policy, Jodie. I'll just say we had a lovely time at the disco, and I'm considering ballroom dancing as a career. Now that I've seen how exciting it is.'

I don't say anything; Shiny's my best mate, and sometimes you simply have to go along with what your best mate says, no matter how mad it is.

'Your hands are like *ice*, Pod!' Virginia is suddenly squeezing them tight. 'They're *freezing*.'

I'm so shocked to be holding hands with her in public, I forget to be shocked.

'Yours are as warm as toast.' They are. I squeeze them as I look into Virginia's dark eyes. 'And if we didn't thank you for hauling our butts out of there, well, *thanks*. I mean, I think we would've made it, anyway. But it would've been quite bad if we didn't. Like, we'd be twenty metres underwater.'

'Yep,' says Shine. 'And that would be a problem. Anyway, Sugar Bix bubblegum anyone? It's got special titanium grains designed to take the enamel off your teeth so they're whiter and brighter and stronger for longer.'

No one wants Sugar Bix bubblegum, not even Shine. He gives it to the seagulls.

'The great thing about you two girls,' he adds, 'is that you're like our best mates, except chicks. You're brave, too. And you're both so pretty I can't even tell which one is the prettiest. I mean, sometimes I think it's Jodie by a mile, then no, I think it's Virginia. Then I just give up and think you're both beautiful.'

As we let that sink in, we look across the channel to the city. And I'd be quite happy, I must say, to sit here holding Virginia's hands for the next two weeks.

'We gotta do stuff like this more often,' I blurt out. 'All of us. Together. Because today's been such a great day. I don't want it to end.'

'Well, it will end.' Shiny nods. 'But tomorrow'll be even better, Poddy, because Sundays are *always* sunny.'

I laugh. 'That's a good theory, Shine,' I say. 'It might even be right.'

'It's not, Pod.' Shiny grins. 'I just said it to make you laugh.'

Which is why, because he's the craziest dude

in Sockby, I'd go on just about any – well, nearly any – adventure that Morris 'Shiny-Boy' Diamond could ever come up with.

'Anyway, Poddy,' Shine adds. 'You know them old railway trolleys with the handles you push and pull to make 'em go? Well, I know where one is. And it's not even hardly chained up. We should check it out one day. It's just near a really nice long slope.'

Er . . . sweet!

About David Metzenthen

I wrote this story because I really like genuinely home-made adventures. I also wanted to show that no matter where you grow up (I grew up in a Melbourne suburb), that place will always remain special, and important, to you.